An Arthur Rackham Story Book

The Night Before Christmas

Henny Penny

Dick Whittington

The Pied Piper

Toads and Diamonds

Harrap London

The Night Before Christmas

'Twas the night before Christmas, when all through
   the house,
Not a creature was stirring, not even a mouse;
The stockings were hung by the chimney with care,

In hopes that St Nicholas soon would be there;
The children were nestled all snug in their beds,
While visions of sugar-plums danced in their heads;
And mamma in her kerchief, and I in my cap,
Had just settled our brains for a long winter's nap;—
When out on the lawn there arose such a clatter,
I sprang from my bed to see what was the matter.

Away to the window I flew like a flash,
Tore open the shutters and threw up the sash.
The moon on the breast of the new-fallen snow,
Gave the lustre of midday to objects below,
When, what to my wondering eyes should appear,
But a miniature sleigh and eight tiny reindeer,
With a little old driver, so lively and quick,
I knew in a moment it must be St Nick.

More rapid than eagles his coursers they came,
And he whistled and shouted, and called them by
   name:
"Now, *Dasher!* now, *Dancer!* now, *Prancer!* and
   Vixen!
On, *Comet!* on, *Cupid!* on, *Donner* and *Blitzen!*
To the top of the porch! to the top of the wall!
Now dash away! dash away! dash away all!"

As dry leaves that before the wild hurricane fly,
When they meet with an obstacle, mount to the sky;
So up to the house-top the coursers they flew
With the sleigh full of toys and St Nicholas too.
And then, in a twinkling, I heard on the roof
The prancing and pawing of each little hoof—
As I drew in my head, and was turning around,

Down the chimney St Nicholas came with a bound.
He was dressed all in furs from his head to his foot,
And his clothes were all tarnished with ashes and
  soot;
A bundle of toys he had flung on his back,
And he looked like a pedlar just opening his pack.
His eyes – how they twinkled! his dimples – how
  merry!

His cheeks were like roses, his nose like a cherry!
His droll little mouth was drawn up like a bow,
And the beard on his chin was as white as the snow;
The stump of a pipe he held tight in his teeth,
And the smoke it encircled his head like a wreath;
He was chubby and plump, a right jolly old elf;
And I laughed when I saw him, in spite of myself;
A wink of his eye and a twist of his head

Soon gave me to know I had nothing to dread;
He spoke not a word, but went straight to his work
And filled all the stockings; then turned with a jerk,
And laying his finger aside of his nose,
And giving a nod, up the chimney he rose.

He sprang to his sleigh, to his team gave a whistle
And away they all flew like the down of a thistle.
But I heard him exclaim, ere he drove out of sight,
"Happy Christmas to all, and to all a good night!"

Clement C. Moore

Henny Penny

There was once a great big chestnut tree grow-
ing in a field where a lot of hens and chickens
lived. One day a little yellow chicken called
Chicky-Wicky was standing under the tree, and
a prickly green chestnut fell *plop* on to her back.

'Oh,' thought Chicky-Wicky, 'the sky is falling! I must run and tell everyone!'

So she ran, and she ran, until she met a pretty speckled hen called Henny-Penny.

'Henny-Penny,' cried Chicky-Wicky, all out of breath, 'I feel *so* excited, the sky is tumbling down! A piece of it fell on my back just now!'

'We must let the King know about this at once,' returned Henny-Penny.

So she and Chicky-Wicky ran, and ran, until they met Ducky-Wucky.

'Ducky-Wucky,' cried Henny-Penny, 'the sky is tumbling down – a piece of it fell on Chicky-Wicky's back just now – and we're going to tell the King.'

'I'm coming too,' said Ducky-Wucky.

And the three birds ran, and ran, till they met Goosey-Woosey.

'Goosey-Woosey,' cried Henny-Penny, 'the sky is tumbling down – a piece of it fell on Chicky-Wicky's back – and we're all on our way to tell the King about it.'

'I'm coming too,' said Goosey-Woosey.

And the four birds ran, and ran, until they met Turkey-Wurkey.

'Turkey-Wurkey,' cried Henny-Penny, 'haven't you heard the news? The sky is tumbling down – a great big piece of it fell on Chicky-Wicky's back – and we are on our way to let the King know about it.'

'I'm coming too,' said Turkey-Wurkey.

And the five birds ran, and ran, till they met Foxy-Woxy.

'Foxy-Woxy,' cried Henny-Penny, 'the sky is tumbling down – a great big piece fell on Chicky-Wicky just now – and we are all on our way to tell the King about it!'

'Dear me,' said Foxy-Woxy, 'I am sure his Majesty will be much interested. Do you know where he lives?'

'Oh, yes,' said Henny-Penny, 'he lives in a silver castle with a roof of gold!'

'Oh, no,' returned Foxy-Woxy, 'not at all – you are *quite* mistaken, Henny-Penny. He lives in a beautiful palace underground. I often go to see him there. So I know the way well.'

'Oh, do show *us* the way!' cried the five birds.

'With pleasure,' said Foxy-Woxy, smiling under his red whiskers.

'This is the way,' he said and Chicky-Wicky, and Henny-Penny, and Ducky-Wucky, and Goosey-Woosey, and Turkey-Wurkey all kept close behind him, and followed where he led, as he had told them to.

And Foxy-Woxy led them into his own deep hole in the side of the hill, and I am sorry to say that not one of them ever came out again.

Dick Whittington

Hundreds of years ago Dick Whittington, the son of two poor peasants, decided to go to London where he had heard that everyone was rich, and where even the streets were paved with gold. It was a long, long walk and by the time he reached London he could scarcely stand. As he looked sadly around him, for although he had seen some rich people most of the Londoners seemed very poor, he had one consolation. He had found a faithful friend – a cat!

While Dick dozed, exhausted, on a doorstep

the cat went off to find an evening meal of mice. Before long Dick was awakened by a well-to-do man who asked him what he was doing there. Dick told him how far he had come, and the man asked him if he would like to earn a little money in his kitchen.

"Oh yes, Sir" said Dick, "I will work very hard – but, Sir, can I keep my cat? He is my only friend, and he is a very good mouser, Sir!"

"Well, my cook will be glad of that" said the man with a laugh. He summoned a servant and said that Dick and his cat should be taken in, and thus began Dick's wonderful story. His new master was a wealthy merchant and very kind, but this did not mean that Dick did not have to work very hard. During the day the cook had him trotting about ceaselessly, and by

the time Dick got up to his little bedroom with his cat, he was ready for a nice long sleep. Indeed, after a few days he felt so tired that he thought he would be better off in his little village, but he had only got a few miles when, as he sat to rest, he heard Bow Bells ringing merrily. It seemed that they were speaking to him and saying:

"Turn again Whittington,
Thrice Lord Mayor of London"

So he decided not to run away after all, and as it was very early in the morning he was able to creep in quickly and start doing his usual work without anyone noticing he had been out, and that very day his master sent for him. He was going to sail abroad and asked Dick to come with him. Dick was delighted, for he had never been on a ship. He was even more delighted when he heard that he was was asked to bring his cat because it would be useful to catch the mice that always scurry about ships.

Within a few weeks they had reached the coast of Barbary and the merchant went ashore to sell to the local King. When he sat down for a meeting the merchant was amazed to see mice dashing about and seizing bits of food during meals. He asked the King if he would like to get rid of the mice, and the King could hardly believe his ears when the merchant said he could do this quite easily. Later that day the merchant asked Dick to bring his cat to the Palace and to the astonishment of all the cat caught or frightened away all the mice in the Palace. The King asked Dick if he might keep the cat but Dick politely said that this was not possible. So the King said "Well, at least you will let me give you a reward," and to Dick's pleasure he was given a sack of valuable jewels before sailing home.

Back in London Dick now found himself rich, and the merchant was so pleased that he asked Dick if he would like to marry his daughter Alice.

So Dick could now hardly believe all the wonderful things that were happening to him.

He was such a modest young man that everyone liked him and the merchant made him a partner in his business. His fame began to spread throughout London and ten years later he was made Lord Mayor, and knighted by the King.

By that time the cat that had brought such fame to Dick was getting very old and was no longer a good mouser. But Dick made sure that his dear cat was treated royally. To the end of his days he was given a beautiful cushion to sit on and fed upon dishes that were fit for the most exalted courtier. Lucky cat! – and lucky Dick to have such a cat!

The Pied Piper

The people of Hamelin had much to make them happy – a pleasant town, with a deep-green river running through it, cosy gabled houses, flowering meadows, and plenty of rosy-cheeked little boys and girls to go and pick the flowers on fine days. But the people of Hamelin had also something to make them very far from happy, and that was the vast number of rats which insisted upon running about everywhere. These rats were of all colours and sizes that rats *can* be, black, white, brown, and grey; some no bigger than mice and some as large as puppies.

And they did a tremendous amount of damage, for they nibbled and munched everything they could reach, and the luckless people of Hamelin could never think of a way to get rid of these unwelcome guests.

'They fought the dogs and killed the cats,
 And bit the babies in the cradles,
And ate the cheeses out of the vats,
Made nests inside men's Sunday hats,
And even spoiled the women's chats
 By drowning their speaking
 With shrieking and squeaking.'

Then one fine day the sound of a pipe was heard in the great open market-square before the main church, and the merchants who ran out to hear the music saw that the piper was a very queer-looking fellow indeed, long and lank, with a swarthy skin and mysterious, mocking green eyes. But the oddest thing about him was his dress, which was of two colours, scarlet and yellow, like the dress of some court fool.

As the people gathered round him, the piper stopped piping and began to sing,

> 'Who lives shall see
> That I am he,
> The man who can catch rats!'

When they heard the words of the song the people were much excited.

'Take him to the Mayor and the Town Council!' they cried all together. Now at that very moment the Mayor and the Town Council happened to be holding yet another meeting to discuss the plague of rats with which Hamelin was afflicted. The piper, followed by the chattering crowd, was brought before them.

'Are you a ratcatcher?' asked the Mayor.

'I am he who can catch rats,' returned the stranger.

'You have come to the right place, if you want a job,' said the Councillors.

'So I understand.'

'I am willing,' said the stranger, 'to clear Hamelin of rats before sunset. But you must pay me a silver florin for every rat.'

'Done!' said the Mayor, finely. 'A bargain's a bargain. You shall receive a florin a head.'

'So be it. The deed will be done at moonrise. I advise the people of Hamelin to remain indoors while I am at work. But there is no reason why they should not look out of their windows. Till moonrise, good sirs!'

At moonrise the piper appeared in the market-place again, and at the sound of his pipe the heads were thrust from every window for a mile round. At first he played slowly and softly, but soon the tune became swift and gay, the sort of tune that sets people tapping their heels and longing to dance. Then the people heard another sound beside the music of the pipe – a

pattering, creaking, scampering sound, that grew louder and louder the longer the piper played. And from every house and cellar and barn, from every cupboard and garret and bin, a great army of rats came pouring into the market-place, all the rats of Hamelin.

The piper looked round, and saw that they were all there. Then, still piping, he set off toward the deep green river that runs through the town. The rats followed hard upon his heels.

On the brink of the river he paused, removed his pipe from his lips, and pointed to the middle of the flood, where the current ran strongest.

'In you go!' he said to the rats.

And in they went, one after another, by dozens, by scores, by hundreds. It was after midnight when the last rat of all reached the river's brink, and he was the first to pause before plunging in. A wise old rat he was, the largest of them all.

So the wise old rat leapt into the river, and vanished at the same spot where the rest of his tribe had gone down. The piper thereupon

returned to his inn, and the townspeople to their beds.

There was peace in Hamelin that night – no crunching, no scuffling, no pattering, no creaking under the floor or behind the wainscot.

The next morning the Town Council met in the Town Hall, rejoicing loudly at the success of the pied piper. A few of the Councillors looked rather grave; they were thinking of the silver florins! But most of them believed in the wisdom of the Mayor, and you may be sure that he believed in it himself, most firmly. 'Trust me!' he said, whenever anyone seemed anxious.

The Council had not long been met together when the piper presented himself before them.

'The rats of Hamelin are gone,' declared he, 'I *could* tell you where, but I will *not* tell. It is enough for you to know that there were nine hundred and ninety nine thousand, nine hundred and ninety nine, and that not one of them will return. Now let us settle the score. You know our bargain.'

'Of course I do,' said the Mayor. 'A silver florin a head. By all means. Certainly. *But where are the heads?*'

'The heads!' repeated the piper, angrily. '*The heads!* If you want them you can go and look for them. I have told you how many there were.

That is all that concerns you and me now.'

'Dear me, no!' cried the Mayor, 'A bargain is a bargain, Master Piper!'

And all the Councillors repeated after him, 'A bargain is a bargain, you know!'

'You have broken *your* part of the agreement,' said the Mayor, 'so, of course, you cannot hold us to *ours*. But we do not wish to appear ungrateful. Here are fifty florins.'

'I will not take your fifty florins,' returned the piper, in a stern voice, while his green eyes glinted fiercely. 'You shall pay me yet – but not in money. Farewell, you wise Councillors of Hamelin!'

'Ha, ha!' laughed the Councillors.

The next day was a Sunday, and all the townsfolk set off for church. They did not take their children with them to the first service of the day, but they looked forward to being welcomed by their rosy-cheeked little boys and girls on their return, and to eating their first Sunday dinner for many years which had not been nibbled beforehand by those wretched rats.

The service was over and all the fathers and mothers went rustling home in their Sunday clothes, but their houses seemed strangely dull and quiet. No little faces peeping out of the windows, no little feet scampering down the stairs, no little voices calling them to make haste, for it was almost dinner time!

'Where are our children?'

Soon all the people were asking each other that question, and hunting high and low, and calling the children by name to come forth from their hiding-places, for their joke had lasted long enough.

Presently some of the people who had gone to seek for the lost children in the meadows at the foot of a great hill on the outskirts of the town met a little lame boy, limping homeward on his crutches, and weeping bitterly. And from him they learned what had happened to the rest.

While all the grown-ups were at church, he said, the children heard the sound of the pied piper's pipe in the market-place, and ran out so that they might hear better. Never was such sweet music! Soon they all began to dance and sing, crowding round the piper, and clinging to his scarlet and yellow sleeves. When he began to march toward the meadows at the foot of the great hill, they all followed him, skipping and jumping, and keeping time to the merry airs he played. But when he reached those meadows, he did not stop. He went straight toward the mountain, and all the children followed. And when he reached the mountain he did not stop. He went straight on, and the mountain opened, and he walked into the mountain, and all the children followed. All, that is to say, except the little cripple. He could not run as fast as the others, and by the time he reached the mountain, the gap had closed again.

Toads and Diamonds

There was once upon a time a widow who had two daughters. The elder was so much like her both in appearance and in nature that whoever looked upon the daughter saw the mother. They were both so disagreeable and proud that there was no living with them.

The younger, who was the very picture of her father for courtesy and sweetness of temper, was also one of the most beautiful maidens ever seen.

But amongst other things, this poor child was made twice a day to fetch water from a spring above a mile and a half from the house, and bring home a pitcher full of it. One day as she was at the fountain there came to her a poor woman, who begged of her to let her drink.

"Ay, with all my heart, Goody," said this pretty little girl.

The good woman, having drunk, said to her, "Thou art so very pretty, my dear, and so good and mannerly, that I cannot help giving thee a gift." For this was a fairy, who had taken the form of a poor country-woman to see how far the civility and good manners of this pretty maiden would go. "I will give thee this gift," said the fairy, "that at every word thou speakest there shall come from thy mouth either a flower or a precious jewel."

When the little maiden came home her mother scolded her for staying so long at the fountain.

"I beg thee to pardon me, Mother," said the poor girl, "for not making more haste." And as she spoke there came out of her mouth two lovely roses, two pearls, and two diamonds.

"What can this be?" said her mother, in amazement. "I really do believe that pearls and diamonds are falling from the girl's mouth! My dear! How can this be?"

Now this was the very first time she had called her "my dear."

Then the little maiden told her what had happened at the fountain in the forest, and all the time she spoke numbers of diamonds and pearls kept on dropping from her mouth.

"This is wonderful!" cried her mother. "I

pearls and the diamonds that dropped from her mouth. He desired her to tell him the whole story, and when he had heard it he lifted her on to his horse and took her with him to the palace of the King his father, and there he married her.

must send thy sister there also. Fanny, Fanny, come here! Look what drops from thy sister's mouth when she speaks! Dear, wouldst not thou be glad to have the same gift bestowed on thee too? Thou hast nothing else to do but go and draw water from the fountain, and when a poor old woman appears and asks thee for a drink to give it to her very civilly."

And she had to go, grumbling all the way, taking with her the best silver tankard.

She no sooner reached the fountain than she saw coming out of the wood a lady splendidly dressed, who asked to drink.

"Am I come hither, pray," said the proud, saucy slut, "to serve thee with water? Dost thou think my fine silver tankard was brought for that? However, if thou hast a fancy thou canst fill it thyself and drink."

"Thou art not over and above mannerly," said the fairy, without showing that she was at all angry. "Well, then, since thou hast so little breeding and art so disobliging the gift I will bestow on thee is that at every word thou speakest there shall spring from thy mouth a snake or a toad." At this she vanished, and the girl went off home.

So soon as her mother saw her coming she cried out, "Well, my child?"

"Well, Mother?" answered the pert little hussy, and out of her mouth there jumped two vipers and two toads.

"Mercy!" cried her mother. "What is this I see? Oh, it's that wretch your sister who has caused all this! But she shall pay for it!" And immediately seizing a stick, she ran to beat her. Hearing her angry words, the poor child fled from the house and hid herself among the trees in the forest.

At that moment the King's son, who was on his way home from hunting, rode by the spot where she was hiding, and, seeing her among the bushes and how beautiful she was, he asked her what she did there alone, and why she was crying.

"Alas, sir," she answered, "my mother has driven me out of doors."

And as she spoke the King's son, who had already fallen in love with her beauty, saw the